Twenty-Five Short Stories For The Holidays

Short Stories from Thanksgiving to New Year's Eve

Written by Anthony D'Armata

Cover art by Brianna D'Armata

Copyright © 2023 Anthony D'Armata

All rights reserved.

ISBN: 9798853049093

CONTENTS

1	Too Short	Pg 1
2	Five Dates for the Holidays	Pg 6
3	Turkey and Dressing and Cell Phone	Pg 8
4	My Lucky Day	Pg 9
5	Tree Lot Bedroom	Pg 12
6	Chasing Christmas Spirit	Pg 15
7	As Best I Can Remember	Pg 23
8	Mystery Snowball	Pg 24
9	One Question	Pg 25
10	Monk on Christmas Eve	Pg 28
11	Every Year	Pg 29
12	A Modern St Nicholas Story	Pg 30
13	More Than a Tree	Pg 32
14	Atmosphere	Pg 34
15	Introvert Thinking	Pg 35
16	Christmas Tree Lot Sleepover	Pg 36

17	Change of Mind	Pg 37
18	Christmas Eve for La Befana	Pg 39
19	Alone Among the People	Pg 42
20	Santa Plus One More	Pg 43
21	New Year's for Herbert	Pg 45
22	Noise Outside the Rectory	Pg 56
23	No More Air	Pg 57
24	Endless Possibilities	Pg 58
25	To Dance or Not	Pg 59
	About the Author	Pg 60

INTRODUCTION

I love the holidays, particularly Christmas. Family, friends, Christmas trees, decorations, spiritual matters, movies, and stories. Who doesn't love a favorite Christmas book or movie that is just right for the season? These stories allow us to experience Christmas and the holidays from the pages of a book or a movie or TV screen, which enhances holiday time. Where would we be without them? Year after year holiday creations speak to us and beacon us to follow.

I hope you like these stories that I enjoyed putting together. May your holidays be filled with family and friends and peace of mind.

Anthony

TOO SHORT

My wife wanted to drag me to this stupid mall. It's December, one week before Christmas–lots of football games on television. I work all week, so on Saturdays I like to stay home and watch football, especially when the Sooners are playing. Marcia insisted that I get away from the television for a while. I mean, does she think I just watch sports on television all the time? Wait…don't answer that…what the heck, I like sports. Give me a good game on TV any day.

Shopping? Who needs it? I went to the mall…about twenty years ago with Marcia. I vowed I'd never go back. We weren't married then. It almost turned out to be our last date. She went into all these stores with me following behind. Each store had a different thing she wanted, so the packages started to pile up. When we left, she was carrying packages with both hands as was I. Need I say it was during the Christmas season? I was bored. I wanted to leave after about ten minutes. When it turned into two hours, I was bored and tired. After three hours I was bored and tired and angry. We had a big argument about it. Marcia said she would never ask me to go to the mall again. That was twenty years ago. She has never asked me to go back to the mall…until now.

Marcia said she wanted me to get out of the house. I'll admit I've been watching a lot of football lately, but it's the season for it. I don't think she was trying to be mean; she was concerned that I was isolating myself too much. I wasn't becoming anti-social or anything. I just love a good game.

"No. You know what happened twenty years ago," I said.

"Bill, you've got to get away from that television." I could tell in her voice she was concerned. "You don't get out enough."

"I like TV, especially when a game is on. You know that."

"I promise it will be different this time. Malls are different than they were twenty years ago. Now, I haven't asked you to go with me in all these years. I think it will do you some good to get out."

"Do they still have stores? Will I have to stand around holding packages?"

"Stores, yes. But I promise you won't have to stand around and hold packages. I have a plan," she said.

I won't have to hold packages. She has a plan. I was weakening.

Anyway, we went to the mall. We split. No, we didn't split up as in divorce, but we went our own ways, and we were going to meet up in an hour: That was her plan. She would go and do her shopping, and I was free to roam. Big deal. What's there to see in a mall? Nothing but stores if you ask me. And what do stores have? Stuff to buy, mostly clothes, from the looks of it.

This was all new to me. I saw women with packages and teenagers hanging out. There were eating places, from pizza to salads to ice cream. A barber shop…here in the mall? I never knew that. It didn't look like any barber shop I had ever seen. I stood in front of the shop and watched people getting their hair cut. There was a light flashing against the wall. It looked like the kind of light from a TV. *In a barber shop?* I could see the TV images flashing, but I didn't know what they were watching. The people getting their hair cut seemed interested in what was on. A man nearly jumped out of his chair; I heard cheers and even the barbers seemed interested. I was curious what was going on. I went inside.

"May I help you?" the cashier said.

I saw that there was a TV mounted on the wall. "Oh, I was just curious what was on."

My question was answered by the sound of the announcer shouting, *"Touchdown! That was Jones's longest run all year. The score is now tied fourteen to fourteen. We'll be back after this message."* My eyes focused on the game.

I heard electric razors and scissors clipping hair. I rubbed my fingers through my hair. Hmm, my hair *is* getting long. I noticed there were some empty chairs. Why not, I thought. I need a haircut anyway. I've still got some time until I meet up with Marcia.

"I'd like a haircut," I said.

"Right this way, sir," he said. He took me to a chair that had a kind of obscured view of the game.

"Could I have the chair in front?"

"Certainly." He led me to the chair that was centered to the TV. Perfect.

It was a good game. State championship. I was beginning to like this mall scene.

"How would you like your haircut?" the barber asked.

I immediately got interested in the game. "Come on, Murphy, we need some yards. We need a touchdown," I said. "Come on coach, run the sideline pass, deep." I was really getting into the game.

"Sir, I was asking how you would like your haircut," the barber said.

Just then, Murphy threw a short pass—way too short for the first down.

"Short, too short," I said. "Too short."

"Short? Too short?" the barber asked.

"Yeah, too short, way short," I said. Then I grumbled under my breath: "Murphy, we needed yards. Too short."

"Very good, sir. Short."

"Come on defense, stop them now," I said. "Oh, and barber, take your time. No hurry."

The game was great. I didn't realize the barber was finished until he took the apron off of me and blew the hair off with the air hose. I watched the game the entire time the barber was working. I was kind of disappointed that he was finished; the game wasn't over. I walked over to the cashier to pay. It was the first time since I entered the shop that I looked in the mirror. I just stared. I didn't complain, because it all came back to me: The barber asking me how I wanted my haircut and all. Me yelling that the pass was "too short." I kind of smiled; I mean the whole thing is kind of funny in a way. I have about a quarter inch of hair all the way around. It'll grow back.

It was time to meet up with Marcia. I headed that way. Every time I passed a store window, I looked at my haircut. *Short, too short.*

When I met up with Marcia, she dropped her packages. The look on her face said it all. She was not expecting to see what she saw. At least she didn't cry like my mom did when I came home with a burr haircut when I was six. Dad had taken me and read magazines while I was in the barber chair.

Marcia kept staring at me as we walked through the mall. She made a beeline to the barber shop.

"Marcia, I didn't tell the guy to cut off all my hair. At least I don't think I did. I was sitting there and—"

"Wait here," she said. She put her one packages beside me.

She went inside. I didn't think she would start anything with them about my haircut, would she? She didn't seem angry when she went inside. I waited by the window. I saw her notice the TV and then she looked outside the window at me. She and the barber talked for a couple of seconds, then they both looked out at me with smiles that let me know everything was alright. She came back out in a couple of minutes. She picked up her packages and put her arm through mine and we left the mall. I opened the car door for her and put her package in the back seat. Her smile said 'I understand. It's okay.' I liked the smile. I just wish she would have said something. Just then, before she got into the car, she kissed me. She was still smiling.

I never knew the mall could be so good.

FIVE DATES FOR THE HOLIDAYS

I love the holidays. I really do. I love the church services, the music, the cold weather, the decorations, all of it. I love Christmas stories and Christmas movies. So, when the holidays approached, I started thinking about how I could enjoy it even more. How could I make better that which is already great, is what I was thinking.

It was only October 6, and already I was thinking about Christmas. It just happened. I wasn't trying to think about Christmas; it was like I automatically thought about Christmas. I always start thinking about the holidays in October, sometimes September. Really, I do.

I couldn't come up with anything new. At work, I daydreamed about how I could make the holidays even better. Then one day I was watching a ball game on TV when this commercial came on—shaving cream or something. One gal after another comes up to this guy, and each one feels how smooth his face is and smells him. He's got his hair slicked down and this suit on. Each gal is different, each attractive. Something clicked in my mind. That's it! I started on a roll in my mind. I found what I was looking for.

What better way to make the holidays better than a bunch of dates. I planned to go out with five different women between Thanksgiving and New Year's Day. There are concerts, movies, plays, dances, all kinds of things going on in town. Why five? I don't know. Seemed like the right number. I would have my fifth date on New Year's Eve. Start the New Year off right. Hey, I know it sounds planned, so what?

I can just picture myself with a gal named Carly. We're dressed up. We're listening to the symphony, live. Afterwards, we'll go and get a bite.

We'll go to my place or her place, whichever is convenient. Yeah, that's it, Carly with the shoulder-length brown hair.

And, there's the movie theater. I can see myself at the movies with someone named Deb. I'll pick her up at her condo. She looks good in jeans and t-shirt. Her red hair falls gently on her shoulders. We'll sit in the dark theater. I don't know what's on the screen. All I can think about is Deb. The show lets out. We'll drive back to her condo. It'l be the best movie night of my life. Yeah, that'll work.

And then there'll be a night of live theater. I'll call her Connie; Connie with the long, curly, graying hair. She'll have a dress on. She'll laugh at all my jokes–good sense of humor. There'll be lots of fun with Connie.

Sally. Sally will be my down-to-earth gal: nothing fancy, just natural beauty. Her long blonde hair matches with her love-of-nature personality. We'll do some outdoor stuff. We'll take walks.

And then for New Year's Eve, I'll dance the night away with Heather. Tall, dark hair, elegant, that's Heather.

Alas…and now to go out and meet the five women.

TURKEY AND DRESSING AND CELL PHONE

I was going to get my new cell phone after school, for my birthday. All day at school I was looking forward to last period gym class. Three o'clock bell and Mom picked me up and we headed straight to the phone place where I got my new phone. Five days of no school ahead. Thanksgiving break.

I set up my phone that night. The night before Thanksgiving Mom was busy with food prep. I helped with stuff, mostly trash duty.

The house was full on Thanksgiving. My grandparents drove down from Amarillo. I live in Longview with my parents.

"Now, Bobby, I want you to put away your cell phone while Grandma and Grandpa are here."

"But, Mom, I just got it." I loved the new games.

"No buts."

I was in the dining room. The men were in the den watching TV and the women were in the kitchen getting the food ready. I was at the dining room table where the plates were set and the veggies and rolls were on the table. The coast was clear. I pulled out my phone. Just then, I heard Mom walking

toward the table. I panicked. I put my phone in the roll basket and put a napkin over it.

"I see you're not on your cell phone. That's nice," she said.

Just then my phone pinged with the win. Mom and I looked at the roll basket.

"I won!" I said.

"No, you lost," Mom said. She held her hand out as I lifted the napkin and I handed her my phone.

MY LUCKY DAY

I'm supposed to shoot deer? I don't think so. I didn't even want to *hold* a rifle. Uncle Rick started the whole thing. He and my dad were going on their before Thanksgiving deer hunt on Uncle Rick's property in East Texas. I'd almost rather be in Mr. Clarke's boring math class. Almost, I said. Believe me, I was glad for the Thanksgiving holidays. No school for a week.

Uncle Rick handed me a rifle. "Here you go, Ted. That's it. Just hold it like so." The metal and wood felt heavy and cold.

"Thanks, I guess." It felt kind of awkward. Only guns I ever handled were pellet guns when I was ten at summer day camp. I handed it back.

"Aw, come on, Teddy, you might get your first buck this time. You can brag to your buddies at school." Dad loved hunting.

The drive to the property was cold. Uncle Rick didn't believe in turning the heater on. He told me, "...so we can get used to the cold at the deer stand." It took us a good two hours to get there. The cabin was surrounded by a big field and a line of trees where the woods started. Uncle Rick's driveway of oyster shell was softened by the pine straw from the nearby trees. I got out of the truck and heard a bird of some kind--one bird.

There was one path that led to the deer stands. I looked over my surroundings. We stowed some food and gear in the cabin and then headed to the deer stand. They wanted to get right at it.

"Got to whisper, son. Don't want to scare the deer away," Dad said.

This was starting to be okay. Maybe I could get a little peace and quiet while I was here. The mile walk to the deer stand was like a meditation to me: trees all around, quiet, cold weather. I felt like a monk going to prayer time. You know, no talking. Beats all the noise in the hallways at school.

We climbed into our deer stand. Still, more quiet. We'd been there about an hour and a half. I almost fell asleep. Then, Uncle Rick elbowed me, "There he is. Take aim."

I awoke myself from my half-sleep and looked fifteen or twenty yards away. I could see the antlers. His head was focused on something on the ground. I hoisted the rifle. But the thought occurred to me: *If I shoot, my peace and quiet will be broken. But I had to do it. Bragging rights.*

I wasn't expecting the shot to be that loud. The butt of the rifle kicked against my shoulder. I fell back but stayed upright. My shot found its target. The deer tried to run but fell before more than a couple of steps.

"Congrats. You're part of the club now." Uncle Rick smiled.

"Way to go, son. You did it."

I won't tell you about cleaning the deer; it was bad enough watching Uncle Rick and Dad handle that. I'll just say that when he was ready, we hoisted him onto the back of Uncle Rick's pickup. I was starting to feel the accomplishment on the way home. I was a part of the club now. I don't know if I'll go back again next year, but I'm glad I went this time.

When we got home there was the neighbor gal who just moved here in September with her family. I'd seen her at school and around, but we hadn't talked yet. I waved. She came over.

"Hi. I'm Sue."

"Nice to meet you, Sue. Ted. I'm glad we finally met."

"Been hunting?" She eyed the hunting gear and my hunting clothes.

"Yeah, got my first buck today." I pointed to the back of the truck.

"Oh, okay. Way to go."

Just then Dad said. "Ted, why don't you invite your friend over for some deer meat on Friday after Thanksgiving?" Wow. Was I surprised? Dad looking out for me like that. He gave me a wink.

"He was right on with his shot. Only took one shot." Now Uncle Rick bragged.

I could see Sue smiling and taking in all this. I was feeling like the quarterback of the team even though I am not on the team.

"Yeah, for sure. Sue, would you like to—"

"I'd love to." Sue looked radiant.

My lucky day.

TREE LOT BEDROOM

Rob was tired of the whole thing: the music, the shopping, the ads on TV. Christmas was over for him before Thanksgiving. His wife was just getting started. He was relaxed in front of the TV as the game progressed.

"Rob, you have no Christmas spirit. Don't touch that radio. I just now turned it on. They're playing Christmas music 24/7 through the holidays."

"Too early for Christmas. They started before Thanksgiving."

"Really? A football game?" Cindy turned the volume up on the radio.

"Pass the football, Johnson's open. Touchdown. Go Notre Dame!"

"Oh, so you get excited about your alma mater's football game?"

"Why not? Perfect time of year for football. Ref, no way that guy was offsides," Rob said.

"I'm going shopping."

"Huh? Yeah, Cindy, you go shopping."

"Trying to get rid of me?"

"You said you wanted to go shopping."

"Thought maybe you'd like to go. You know...get some Christmas spirit."

"You want me to get some Christmas spirit? I'll tell you what. I'll spend the night at the Christmas tree lot."

"Now you've flipped."

"No, seriously. I'm going down to Busca's tree lot...right after this game."

"Ha. Enjoy your game, Rob. I'm going shopping."

"I'll be gone when you get back."

"Yeah, sure." Cindy left

After the game ended, Rob put down the remote and started packing. *"I'll show her I meant it. She wants to see some Christmas spirit? I'll show her some Christmas spirit. Got my sleeping bag and my backpack. Cell phone? No way. I want it to be just like Christmases when I was a boy in 1974. It'll be just like a campout. Trees all around. Quiet at night. Take me some snacks. There, I'm done packing. Bye, house. See you on Monday. I'll leave a note for Cindy: Hi, Cindy, when you read this I'll be at my home for the evening, Busca's Tree Lot. I'll get me some Christmas spirit and I'll see you in the morning. Hope your shopping went well. Robbie."*

When Rob got to the lot it was crowded. He parked on the next street so Mr. Busca wouldn't see his car when the lot was empty after he closed. Darkness had set in. He wandered to the back and crouched behind a row of husky trees. *"I'll just sneak back here and nobody will be the wiser. Mmm. I love the smell of Christmas trees. A whole night of it. I'll show Cindy I have Christmas spirit. I've got my backpack with snacks."*

The last of the customers left the lot, and Mr. Busca locked the gate and shut out the lights. Immediately, Rob had second thoughts.

"What have I done? It's lonely. I love the smell of pine, but I miss my home and my Cindy. What was that?" Rob picked up a branch for protection. "Who's there?"

He heard rustling and some footsteps outside the gate. He looked over the fence and couldn't believe it: Cindy.

"Oh, Rob, I'll never accuse you of a lack of Christmas spirit again."

Rob smiled and hurried over to the fence.

"Got room for one more around this fort of trees? I brought some snacks and a blanket," Cindy said.

"Here, right over this fence. I didn't know it would be so easy to break into a Christmas tree lot." Rob helped Cindy over the fence.

They made a bed of pine straw. They had privacy (not that there was anyone else there). They had a wall of trees surrounding them in a circle. They slept.

Next morning Mr. Busca opened the gate. Rob and Cindy scurried to get up and blend in to look as though they were customers who had just arrived. They stuffed their blankets into the back packs and at the right moment, they joined in with the crowd filing in to pick out their trees.

"How may I help you?" Mr. Busca stood before them all smiles at the prospect of a sale. "Backpacks? You two look like you've come to stay overnight." Mr. Busca winked at them. Did he know?

"Ha, well, we, um, like to bring food and snacks when we go shopping, um, this looks like a nice tree. What do you think, Cindy?" They both picked up the tree that they had slept with. "We'd like this one."

"Oh I can get you a much better tree than that one," Mr. Busca said. "This one looks like someone slept on it." Again, Mr. Busca winked.

Rob and Cindy smiled and held onto their misshapen and squashed tree. They knew that the only tree for them this year was the one that was bent and misshapen and missing limbs.They wouldn't trade it for any other tree on the lot. "We'll take this one. It's perfect."

CHASING CHRISTMAS SPIRIT

I told my wife I wanted to go shopping with her the day after Thanksgiving. I've been working a lot lately, and I wanted to get out of the house and catch the holiday spirit. I've never been shopping the day after Thanksgiving. I don't go shopping at all.

"You what?" she asked.

"Yes, I'd like to go shopping with you on Friday," I said.

"Don, you hate shopping."

"I know I hate shopping, but I love Christmas. I love the songs, the joy, the movies. I love—"

"Okay, I get it. We'll go shopping on Friday. But, do you know what it's like out there on Friday after Thanksgiving?"

"It's the start of the Christmas season. We can look at Christmas decorations and get something to eat and look at all the new gadgets and buy presents and—"

"Don." She sat down. She hadn't planned on this. I think she had to reconfigure her plans now that I would be going along.

"Karen," I said. "You okay?" She looked upset as though I had done something wrong.

"Yeah. I was just thinking. Isn't there one of those fruit bowl games on TV on Friday?" she asked.

"You mean a bowl game?"

She brightened up at the prospect that I might stay home and watch a football game instead of go shopping with her. "Yeah, one of those bowl games," she said.

"I don't want to stay at home and watch football. I want to go with you."

Thanksgiving Day was typical of our family. Karen's aunt and her uncle and their spouses, Karen's cousin Mary, my sister Peggy and her husband Phil and their two toddlers all joined us for a mid-afternoon turkey and all the trimmings. Karen cooked the turkey and the others brought side dishes. After lunch Phil and I got to talking about the weekend.

"Gonna watch the big game tomorrow, Don?" he asked.

"Well, I'm gonna do it a bit differently this year. I'm going with Karen on the big shopping day." There was a pause. Phil looked at me to try to find some humor in what I was saying. He was waiting for the punchline which never came because I was serious. I broke the silence.

"Really, I'm gonna do it," I said.

"Yeah, right." His face changed to laughter. "You really had me going there. Listen, It's gonna be a great game. Two top quarterbacks—"

"No, Phil, I'm not kidding. I'm going shopping with Karen. Gonna get out there with the people."

"I thought you were kidding." Phil looked around as though he were looking for someone to help out with this awkward conversation. "I just don't get it. You're gonna give up the game to hang with those crazies in the mall?"

"I don't know if we're going to the mall. I just want to get out," I said.

"I've seen how those shoppers behave the day after Thanksgiving. You couldn't pay me to do that. You okay, Don?"

"Sound as can be."

"Okay. I just…I'm surprised, that's all."

Phil didn't say anything the rest of the day. He and I were in the den. We watched a program on the history of the Ivy League. When everyone started to leave, Phil turned to me.

"Don. If you want to come over and watch the game tomorrow, I'll be home. We can—"

"I want to go shopping. I'm fine with that."

Phil looked puzzled.

It was a good Thanksgiving. I had my plan. I was ready. I was excited. I would be doing something different. Break with tradition.

Friday morning made me even stronger in my conviction to go with Karen. I got the feeling that she hoped I would change my mind. I am not sure why she was so against my going with her.

We skipped breakfast. I didn't know what that meant. Is that some sort of tradition that goes with the Friday after Thanksgiving or was Karen trying to throw me a curve that would change my mind? Maybe she thought I would stay home and eat breakfast.

"We'll get something later," I said. I know that those malls have eating places. I saw it on the news one time. And, I've heard Franklin at work talk about his son who works at the pizza place in the mall.

"You might get hungry, Don. Don't you want to stay home, read the paper, have coffee and breakfast, and watch the game?"

"I just want to spend the day with you and be in the Christmas mood."

She stared in disbelief.

I've been staying home on the Friday after Thanksgiving for the eight years that Karen and I have been married. We got married right out of grad school. Karen teaches science at the high school, and I teach geography at community college. We're not intellectuals. I don't mean that as a put down; we just don't hang out with the academic crowd. We love teaching; that's why we're in it. I can't think of anything else I'd want to do for a living. We do things outside of the academic realm on our off time. Karen crochets, paints, cooks, and shops. I like to write short stories, read, and watch sports. We took a dance class this year and learned swing dance. One year we helped build sets at a community theater. So it's not as if we don't do things together; we're active. I guess that's one reason why Karen was surprised that I wanted to go shopping with her; we do stuff together as it is. Also, she knows I hate shopping.

I do hate shopping. But I want to experience the after-Thanksgiving day thing. I've always heard about it on the news on television.

We started out at the mall. I couldn't believe the parking lot was almost full at eleven o'clock in the morning. So far so good. We found a place to park and walked inside. Wow! It's been years since I'd been in a mall. I wasn't regretting it; I just wasn't prepared for the number of people moving about and the three levels of stores. I was surprised but not overwhelmed.

"Okay, where do we start?" I asked.

"It doesn't work that way," Karen said.

"Well, we have to have a plan."

"I just start. I walk into the first interesting store and go at it. I shop," she said.

"Okay, let's do this." I was surprised she was so random about shopping. I just wouldn't go inside a mall and fall into the first store that looked interesting. If I know what I want, I aim for my target. But, I'm game. I'm a newcomer at this. Let her have her "no plan."

She started for a shop that had dresses in the display window. I could see inside the store. There were racks of dresses and underwear and a lot of pink and purple and red.

"Do we have to start here?"

"Now look, that's why I didn't want to do this. Already you are interfering with my day. I'm sorry, Don. I didn't mean to yell. It's just that…look why don't you explore the mall and we'll meet up in an hour and get a bite to eat."

"Okay…I don't know where anything is…I don't see a lot of friendly faces."

"See, I told you it isn't all it's cracked up to—"

"No. I'm not changing my mind. I just didn't know this was how it…I thought this was some kind of winter wonderland where—"

Just then a lady gave me a mean look. I was blocking her entrance into the women's clothing store. I moved out of the way. I needed to sit down. I felt faint.

"Why don't we meet in the center of the mall, over there by the snow village display. Let's say, in an hour." Karen knew her mall.

I looked where she was pointing. I could see in the distance the white of the snow display. "Okay, see you in an hour," I said.

She went into the store. I took a couple of steps. Something wasn't right. I felt weak. I barely made it to a bench.

Relief. I sat and closed my eyes to all the movement and noise. Everyone was talking but it was all a jumble as people passed by. The noise of shoes on the move and the incessant talking drowned out any Christmas music that might have been playing. I opened my eyes and felt better but the noise and movements were still present. People were crisscrossing and kids were screaming. I took some deep breaths, I gained some strength and started walking.

This whole thing wasn't turning out as I had expected. The mall was no paradise, just a haven of stores wanting you to spend your money. They made it attractive to the shoppers, I could tell, but behind the scenes I imagined a battery of calculators, ledgers, managers with sales quotas to meet, disgruntled relations between employee and employer, etc. I was getting pessimistic.

I made my way to the snow village display. There was no real snow but it looked real. There were trees, and ground area covered with white stuff. You couldn't walk on it. I guess it was supposed to get people in the mood for winter and Christmas spending. Santa was sitting in his big chair. The kids and parents in line waited their turn for the traditional visit to Santa.

I kept walking to the big department store at the end of the mall. I took the escalator upstairs. I remember when I was a kid there was always interesting stuff upstairs in the big department store downtown. There were televisions, pets, electronics, appliances, and outdoor stuff. As the escalator ascended I looked downstairs at the mannequins and jewelry and clothing. I had no interest in these things. Upstairs, I saw the furniture department and the televisions. There were recliner chairs. I caught a glimpse of a football game. I gravitated toward this. I hadn't planned on seeing a football game today. I had planned on a day at the mall to get into the Christmas spirit. But here I was, just as I had been doing for the past eight years after Thanksgiving. I was watching a football game on television. Maybe this was it for me. Maybe this was my Christmas spirit and it took me to get out of the house to discover that my Christmas was exactly as I had been doing every year at home. I didn't need to change it.

Too many televisions on at once was confusing. Some had the same football game on and some had movies on and commercials. The different sizes were no help. Each had a slightly different tone of color, more confusion. A salesman was ready to answer any questions in order to make the sale. At home I never have this problem; I have one television with one size and its own tone of color and one channel at a time. I felt dizzy. I looked away. I turned away and left.

The escalator descended this time back to the first floor and into the land of clothes. I left the store. I was back in the mall. Everything was a blur. People, stores, kids yelling, the sound of shoes (hundreds) striking the concrete floor all made for more confusion. I was in a world where I didn't belong. What was I thinking when I decided to do this? I didn't see it coming. Karen was right in trying to convince me to stay home. I bought into the whole Christmas is done "this way" thing.

Ten minutes left until I would meet Karen back at the snow village display. I held onto the wall between stores. I was disoriented. I felt faint again. I tried to focus and walked. I stayed close to the wall. I felt if I let go of the wall I would pass out. I looked down at the floor to take my eyes away from all the movement of people around me. I thought about my den and my television and my hot chocolate and my reclining chair. This gave me the strength to get myself together and move away from the wall. The thought that I would be home soon and back in my den and my computer screen, which held my first draft to my next short story, gave me much needed strength.

I saw in the distance the snow village. There was Karen, my oasis of relief in a desert of confusion. She was where she belonged on the day after the turkey and dressing holiday; I was not. She had several packages with her, some big, some small. She had this shopping thing down. I somehow made my way to her. As I got closer to her I gained my strength. My confusion and despair disappeared as I got closer to her. I zeroed in on her with blinders to the distraction of shoppers to my left, right, and all around. I smiled a giant smile. I knew that this would be my last after-Thanksgiving trip to the mall. I was only too happy to help her with her packages as we made our way out of the mall and to our car and then to home.

I was beaten. The mall beat me.

AS BEST AS I CAN REMEMBER

One of our parishioners came to see me at the rectory the other day. He asked me to tell him the story about St. Nicholas and the fishermen that he rescued. I asked him why he wanted that tale told.

"Father Albert, I am going deep sea fishing with my company. I just want to know for my own peace of mind. I'm terrified to go but I almost have to–the whole department is going."

"Well, Bobby, as best I remember it there were some fishermen out to sea. A storm developed and the sea became rough. The waves tossed the boat around. The men became afraid. They got on their knees and prayed to St. Nicholas. Immediately, there appeared a man with a Bishop's miter and a long white beard. *The Lord is with you, my fine fishermen. I will guide you to shore.'* The waves calmed. The sky cleared. The boat was being guided to shore. The men got back on their knees and thanked St. Nicholas for his intercession.

"That's how I best remember it, Bobby," I said.

"Thank you, Father. That eases my mind. I have to do this thing with my company. The owner of the company has chartered a boat. I don't like boats, but I have to do the company thing."

"Well, you can always invoke St. Nicholas."

MYSTERY SNOWBALL

My dad woke me up and said go look outside. This was out of the ordinary because my dad never woke me early for school. I went and looked out the window and saw nothing but white on the lawns and shrubs. It had snowed overnight. My first snow. My prayers answered.

The first thing I thought was *no school.* I got dressed and joined my neighborhood friends who were filing out of their houses. We stared up and down the street. Nothing but white lawns all over. We hadn't seen anything like this in our town. Oh, maybe they had snow here before, but we were too young to remember the last snow twelve years ago.

The sad part was that it only lasted a day. The next day we were back in school. The snow was melting in the afternoon. Back to algebra, yuck.

There was still some snow around the school the next morning. In between classes there was a snowball or two thrown. Heck, I threw a couple myself. After second period math, I went from the main building to the temporary rooms that are outside. Lots of people take this sidewalk back and forth between classes. I reached down in the grass next to the sidewalk and formed a snowball and let it fly. I didn't aim it at anyone. I just felt like throwing a snowball before it all melted. I wasn't the only one. Only trouble was the snowball hit this guy I didn't even know. I immediately regretted it. He started looking around to see who threw it. He never did find out who threw it; there were snowballs flying all over the place, and there were so many students and teachers passing. He looked around. I played dumb. I felt bad about it afterwards.

ONE QUESTION

Two thirtyish men, Fred and George, were sitting on a bench in the mall while their wives were in the stores. They kept checking their watches. They were seated on the benches for like-minded reasons–they didn't want to be inside the stores. Waiting on these benches was close enough to any store. Closing time couldn't come soon enough for these guys, although they made the best of it. Christmas trees and decorations and lights were everywhere. The latest gadgets and eye catchers were in the store windows. It was 1985 and shopping and the season was alive and thriving in the mall.

Plenty to see: Shoppers of all ages. Some were doing funny things like trying to balance bags and more bags of gifts. One woman had her arms filled with packages and her three kids loaded down with packages.

A man sat down between Fred and George. He had a white beard and a cane; he wasn't elderly. He was dressed in a well-tailored earth tone suit and matching vest. Dapper. He was dressed like something from another era, though he didn't stand out as odd. He smiled and spoke to the two men.

"How are you, gentlemen?"

Both looked startled as they were minding their own business and just wanted to leave as soon as their wives had completed their shopping. But being civilized, they acknowledged the bearded man. "Hello, sir, and how are you?" George asked.

"Hi. Busy place tonight, eh." Fred said.

"I'm here visiting my brother. He works here at the mall." The white-bearded man exuded goodwill.

"I feel for you. It's all we can do to wait for our wives. But we're going out to eat after," George said.

"I see the wives coming out of the store now. Gotta go." Fred stood up.

Both men headed toward their wives exiting the store. They took three steps and were halted in their tracks by the voice of the white-bearded man, "If you see my brother on the way out, tell him you spoke to me."

Both were surprised at this unusual request from a stranger that they didn't know.

Fred was getting annoyed. "Oh? How would we know your brother?

"Yeah, we don't know you or your brother," George said.

The white-bearded man stood up. "You'll find him over at the North Pole setup. Let's just say he's gathering information for his work. Toy requests, you know." The old man winked and sat back down. Fred and George headed toward their wives. As they did, they stopped and looked back. Startled. In a daze. They looked back again. The white-bearded man was nowhere to be seen. Disappeared. They looked at each other again.

Both men met up with their wives and headed toward the parking lot, which meant passing the North Pole exhibit. They stopped and stared at Santa and the line of kids waiting to talk to him.

George had a thought. "Should we tell the Santa guy we saw his--"

"Why not. I'm up for a good laugh. Probably some nutcase. Lots of those around the holidays." Fred grinned.

"Was that guy trying to tell us he's Santa's brother?" George asked.

"Like I said, crazies all over the place. This shopping stuff will do it to you. But hey, let's play along and see what the big guy says."

Their wives were wondering what their husbands were up to.

They reached the Santa chair just as Santa had finished listening to a boy give him his list.

"Hey, Santa. Saw your brother over there. Said to say hello." Fred and George laughed as they knew this whole thing to be a joke. They walked off holding back laughs. Their wives couldn't believe what just happened.

But before they got two steps away, Santa said to Fred and George. "Thanks for letting me know. Glad he's in town. Merry Christmas."

Both men halted. All semblance of smiles and laughter was gone. The joke was over. Each paused and looked at each other with deer-in-headlights expressions and grabbed hold of their wives hands and left the mall. They didn't look back.

When they got to their cars, they had one question for their wives: "Does Santa have a brother?"

MONK ON CHRISTMAS EVE

I couldn't sleep—didn't want to. I got up from my bed and walked to the edge of the yard near the woods. The stars were bright against the backdrop of a clear midwest night sky. Morning prayer would be soon. I thought of home. I thought of my friends and family.

I went back to the abbey
and to my room. My brother monks were asleep. Father Bernard was getting the altar ready for Christmas Eve mass. The monastery was about to be awake. It was 3:00 am.

EVERY YEAR

I sold a lot of Christmas trees today. I run a Christmas tree lot. Have for thirty-five years. Some of my customers know me. They only see me once a year, but we're like old friends. And there are always new people and new families buying their first tree together. Just think, I'm the one who gets to sell them their trees that will be in their family pictures forever. They tell me about their Christmas traditions. I think they tell me because they want to hear it themselves. They are so looking forward to the holidays that they have to share it when they get their tree. I feel like I'm a part of their lives, in a way. My trees will be decorated in their dens and living rooms when their families and friends come over.

I always say it's my last year, but the smell of Christmas trees always calls me back. And I think I'm reluctant to leave because I'll miss all the people I get to see and meet. Always happy people–I've never seen an unhappy face picking out a Christmans tree. I'm not in it for the money; I'll never get rich doing this.

But, there's a sad part to this business. When all the trees are gone and Christmas is over, all I have left is a lot full of pine needles. No one sees that. I sweep them up and then it's an empty lot. Until next year.

A MODERN ST NICHOLAS STORY

Nicholas's wealthy parents died when he was a boy. He inherited their fortune, but he was not interested in the money. He mostly spent his time at church and in prayer.

In his twenties he learned about a family with three lads who fell on hard times. The boys were close in age: seven, eight, and ten. Their parents loved them but could not provide the necessities, let alone anything beyond that. The boys had to watch as other boys got toys and bicycles and games for Christmas. Other boys told them of their summer homes, lake houses, and vacations.

Nicholas learned of this.

The dad worked as best he could. The mom took care of the house and tried to stretch their meager finances as best she could. Nicholas wanted to help, but he didn't want the accolades. He didn't want them to know…but how could he give to them without their knowing?

Nicholas was about to enter a monastery to follow his vocation, but before he did, he would have to get rid of all his worldly possessions, including the fortune his parents left him. He went to see a lawyer.

He had the lawyer draw up papers to bequeath everything to the family with the three boys. Anonymously. This would take place the day after he entered the monastery. The only thing he asked was that the lawyer contact him and let him know how the family was doing with their newfound wealth.

Nicholas began his novitiate. And lived his vocation of prayer.

As directed the lawyer sent the papers through and the family learned of their good fortune. The family got out of poverty and lived well, but frugally. There was no extravagant spending. Every night at the dinner table, time was spent in thanking God for their bountiful life and the security of their future. The boys went on to university and to successful lives of family and commerce. The lawyer sent Nicholas a yearly letter and let him know that the family was doing well.

The family wanted to express their gratitude for their good fortune, but they didn't know where to start. Through the years they have tried to get the lawyer to open the books and let them know. As of this writing, they still do not know.

MORE THAN A TREE

I didn't know what kind of tree I'd get. The tree lot was huge. I love the smell of the trees all in one place in the tree lot. There were families walking around. It's lonely when you are single and looking for a Christmas tree.

"May I help you, sir?" The sales lady was in her 30s, strawberry blonde hair, blue jeans.

"Yes, I'm looking for a tree. Don't know what to get. It's just me."

"I know what you mean. I'm single too," she said.

I saw one that would be just right for my place. "I like this one." It was a medium height tree. "Not too big."

"Good choice," she said.

"One other thing. Will you come over and help me decorate?" I asked. I couldn't believe my forwardness. I just blurted it out. I had never done anything like that before. Too lonely, too long, I guess.

We decorated the tree at midnight. In the morning we had eggs, biscuits, and coffee.

Introvert Thriving

I just want out. I want the semester to be over. Last day before Christmas vacation starts. Two weeks without school. No teachers. No loud-mouth football jocks shouting up and down the halls.

Lunch time. At least I'm halfway there. I have study hall after lunch. Good ol' study hall where I can doodle and think and read and daydream and go to the library.

I'll grab some rolls and milk in the cafeteria and go outside and eat alone by the benches. Maybe I'll sit on those benches today. Why not? I don't have to stand and eat out in the open.

Let's see. Hey, nobody at the benches. Great, I'll grab some quiet time. These benches are cool. Shade trees. Quiet. No one else around...oops, I spoke too soon.

"Hi, may I sit here?" She had blonde hair and was wearing blue jeans.

"Sure. I was just having my lunch." I looked again. *Is this a girl coming up to me and talking? Me, the non-athlete. Me, the non-superstar. Me, the non-jock.*

"Thanks. My name's Julie."

"Oh, nice to meet you, Julie. I'm Skip." *Man, I can't believe this is happening. This is great. I'm feeling good about this.*

"Skip, nice to meet you."

I hope Christmas vacation never comes.

ATMOSPHERE

I'm at the tree lot. Man, it smells good here. All that pine. Christmas music is playing in the background. Families are walking around trying to find just the right tree for their living room. Everyone's happy.

I'm not here to find a tree. I just like the atmosphere.

INTROVERT THINKING

I just want out. I want the semester to be over. Last day before Christmas vacation starts. Two weeks without school. No teachers. No loud-mouth football jocks shouting up and down the halls.

Lunch time. At least I'm halfway there. I have study hall after lunch. Good ol' study hall where I can doodle and think and read and daydream and go to the library.

I'll grab some rolls and milk in the cafeteria and go outside and eat alone by the benches. Maybe I'll sit on those benches today. Why not? I don't have to stand and eat out in the open.

Let's see. Hey, nobody at the benches. Great, I'll grab some quiet time. These benches are cool. Shade trees. Quiet. No one else around...oops, I spoke too soon.

"Hi, may I sit here?" She had blonde hair and was wearing blue jeans.

"Sure. I was just having my lunch." I looked again. Is this a girl coming up to me and talking? Me, the non-athlete. Me, the non-superstar. Me, the non-jock.

"Thanks. My name's Julie."

"Oh, nice to meet you, Julie. I'm Skip." Man, I can't believe this is happening. This is great. I'm feeling good about this.

"Skip, nice to meet you."

I hope Christmas vacation never comes.

CHRISTMAS TREE LOT SLEEPOVER

I like the smell of Christmas trees, but I didn't want to stay there all night. But I did. How can you get trapped in a Christmas tree lot? Let me explain.

I wanted a tree for my apartment. I was going to have a party on Saturday, the twenty-third. I had some decorations but needed a tree.

The lot was huge. Like a car dealer's lot. In fact it used to be a car dealer's lot. The guy selling the trees took me to the back of the lot where the smaller trees were. The tree I wanted had to be small to fit into my apartment. All the small trees were in the back of the lot. He left me there to look them over while he went to help other customers. I kept going farther and farther back. The trees seemed to never end. I guess I didn't realize how long I had been there. The lights at the front of the lot went out and the last car pulled out. I was alone.

There is an eleven foot fence around the place. I chose not to climb. I laid down and fell asleep.

CHANGE OF MIND

Last class before Christmas vacation. Band class. We played some holiday songs which fitted the mood I was in. There's something about that last day of school before Christmas vacation. It's like I know I won't have to come to school tomorrow. I can stay home. Don't have to feel uncomfortable at school for a whole two weeks. We'll go to my uncle and aunt's house on Christmas Eve. They live in this new subdivision about fifty miles away. It's so new there are no paved streets, and there are woods. Heck, there aren't even any houses…just kidding. We'll stay there overnight and have Christmas there.

I didn't mind my classes today. Even old Mr. Murphy and his math class, which I hate. I like old Mr. Baldwin's biology class. He's kind of funny. Short and bald. He likes to joke around. Not bad for a teacher.

Cold outside. Might snow. That would top it off. Make the last day before Christmas vacation that much better.

I put my sax case on the shelf and got my backpack. Mr. Saunder told us to have a nice vacation. I like old Saunder. I like band class too. Just as I was about to walk out of the room and into the world of vacation, this gal named Valerie came up to me and said have a nice Christmas. I've been wanting to talk to Valerie all semester and now she talks to me when I'm about to leave for two weeks?

She was putting her clarinet in the case. "Hi."

"Oh, hi." I was kind of in shock.

"I like the way you play sax," she said. "Sounds smooth."

"Thanks."

"I sit right in the clarinet section, right in front of you."

"Oh, okay. We've got a great band and director."

"Yeah, Mr. Saunder is the best," she said.

Valerie winked at me as we went our separate ways. Girls kill me when they wink. I mean, a girl doesn't even have to say anything. Just that wink is enough to say it all. That kills me every time.

So, I left school for my two week vacation. *Vacation?* Wait a minute. I'll be gone from school for two weeks. I just started talking to this girl Valerie. What if she forgets me during vacation? This is torture.

I can't wait for vacation to be over and get back to band class and school.

And Valerie.

CHRISTMAS EVE FOR LA BEFANA

You may be familiar with La Befana and the Epiphany and what happened when the magi invited her to join them in search of the Child. She was too busy with her housekeeping. Later, she regretted not going with them and to this day she is in search of the baby Jesus. She goes from house to house and leaves all the good children treats and toys in hopes that one of them will be the Christ Child. This is a story about La Befana on Christmas Eve.

La Befana lived in a small town in Sicily. She was busy baking bread and cookies in December. And of course she was busy with her ever present housekeeping. Father Francesco came by every Monday, Wednesday, and Friday for the bread for the needy and the orphan children.

It was December 1 and Father stopped by for the bread. "Thank you, Befana. Won't you join us for mass and our Christmas party on Christmas Eve?" He asked.

"Oh, no. No thank you, Father. I have to bake bread and cookies. And take care of the house."

"God bless you, Befana." He made the sign of the cross and left.

Christmas Eve arrived and La Befana was still baking. There was a knock at the door. "Who can that be? I have to bake. No time for company."

Her dress had flour on it and her hands were dusty white when she opened the door. There stood three men wearing brown monk's habits. "Good day, Befana. I am Brother Antonio and this is Brother Mario, and Brother Salvatore. Father Francesco has asked us to come and see if we can escort you to mass and the Christmas party tonight."

"No, I have to bake. No time for celebrations."

"The party will be after midnight mass. The townsfolk and children will be there," Brother Antonio said.

"Midnight mass? Midnight? I have to sleep after baking. No time for celebration."

"We are celebrating the birth of the Christ Child."

"No time for--" La Befana suddenly was filled with wonder and delight. "The Christ Child?"

"Yes. Please join us."

La Befana had a change of heart and mind. "I can bake anytime. I want to spend this time in celebration. I will bring my fresh baked bread and cookies. I want to share them and be with the townsfolk so I can see them enjoy my bread. I want to delight in the happiness of the children when they taste my cookies."

La Befana put her fresh baked bread and cookies in baskets, and added some olives and cheese. She cleaned her hands, and got her shawl. The brothers helped her carry the baskets down the road to the church. "And to think I almost missed it. Baking can wait till I get back. For now it's time to be with the townsfolk and children. It's time to welcome the Christ child."

La Befana had a wonderful time at the celebration of mass and the party after. Before that night, she had not experienced the joy of the townsfolk and children as they enjoyed her baked goods. She had always been baking and taking care of her house on Christmas Eve.

She sat on the front pew at mass. The party after mass was in the meeting room adjacent to the church. Her bread and olives and cheese were served along with some wine that someone brought. The cookies brought joy to the children.

When she got home, in the early morning hours, she looked around. There was flour on the table and even on the floor. "I will clean it up tomorrow. But tonight I shall be happy in the joy of the townsfolk and the joy of the birth of the Christ child."

Before she got in bed she resolved to always answer the door and be ready for what is to come. "Who knows what opportunities I might miss if I'm too busy baking. The Epiphany is not far away. I will be ready. I must sweep and make a clean and welcoming path outside my door...but, it can wait till tomorrow."

Will La Befana be ready for the magi when they come to her house on the Eve of the Epiphany? Or will she be too busy with her baking and housekeeping to follow them to the baby?

ALONE AMONG THE PEOPLE

I got off work and went to the mall to see what was happening. I was alone, single. The mall was full of people and noise and music and laughter. It wasn't Black Friday, but it was the day before Christmas Eve. I saw a little boy with his mom; they went inside a toy store. Two teenage girls went inside a clothing store that had bright lights and pop music.

The mall had an ice skating rink. There were skaters and skating music. I stood outside the rink and felt the frost from the ice as the skaters went round and round. There were restaurants, an ice cream parlor, and cafes. I thought the hamburgers and Mexican food smelled good.

I left. I felt so alone among all those people.

SANTA PLUS ONE MORE

Everybody's busy here at the North Pole, which is good. We will get the toys out tonight as always. Got a good crew here. The reindeer are ready, well-fed and well-rested. I think I will go inside and have a hot chocolate with Mrs. Claus.

"Hi, dear, want a hot chocolate?" she asked as I walked into the room.

"Just what I had in mind. Snowing again, just like we like it," I said.

"Everything on schedule?"

"As always. The elves are finishing up the last of the basketballs and putting the finishing touches on the doll houses. Lots more kids this year," I said.

"I think I'd like to go along this year," Mrs. Claus said.

"Go along? Claire, are you sure you want to go? I mean, we travel a long way in a short time."

"Yes, I'd like to go with you this year. I'd like to experience the Christmas Eve toy delivery. I'd like to thank those folks at that post office for handling all those letters we get."

"Okay, sure. I just thought you liked to stay here at the Pole and relax while we are out for the Christmas Eve run."

"I do, but this year I want to go."

"Okay, well I think I'll go and inspect the sleigh and make room for one more," I said.

I never thought of bringing Mrs. Claus with me. She always likes to stay put in the quiet after the business of the December preparation.

We took off at our scheduled time. I don't make appearances on Christmas Eve, but I knew it was important to Mrs. Claus this year. We stopped off at the post office in Indiana, and the folks were surprised to see us. We couldn't stay long–had to make the rest of our deliveries before heading back to the North Pole. The only other time I was ever seen on Christmas Eve was that time I came down the chimney and that fellow wrote a poem out of my visit.

I wonder if someone will write a poem about seeing us on Christmas Eve at the post office in Indiana?

NEW YEAR'S EVE FOR HERBERT

Herbert never had a date for New Year's Eve. This year he met someone on Christmas day and asked her out and...wait, I'm getting ahead of the story. Let me just back up and fill you in on the details of what happened on Christmas day and then on New Year's Eve. It was December, several days before Christmas. Herbert was alone, single...

Herbert was wondering what he might do on New Year's Eve. Here it was not even Christmas and already he was thinking about New Year's Eve. He did not want to stay home and watch the ball drop in New York City, on television. He had done that in his twenties, but watching on TV always felt somewhat removed from the fun.

He was invited to spend Christmas with his cousin on the other side of town. His cousin George was married and had an eight year old named Linda and a six year old named Samantha. George and Herbert, now in their thirties, had spent many a holiday together when they were kids.

Herbert had just arrived home from work at the bookstore when the phone rang. He closed his apartment door, put down the grocery bag he was carrying, and answered the phone. It was George.

"Herbie? This is George. How the heck are ya? Haven't seen ya in a while. The reason I'm calling is that Betty and I would like to invite you to join us for Christmas dinner at our house."

"Wow. Yeah, I'd like to see you two and Linda and Samantha. Sure. Yeah. Thanks. I have no plans for Christmas day. Michele and I broke up about a month ago, so it's been kinda lonely."

"Oh. I didn't know about you and Michele calling it quits. Sorry to hear that, cuz." There is a kind of awkward pause. "Well, we look forward to having ya here. Betty is making the dressing recipe that Aunt Martha used to make. Man, we really used to love that dressing. I miss ol' Aunt Martha, God rest her."

"Betty has the recipe?" Herbert asked.

Their Aunt Martha used to make the family favorite Christmas dressing when they were growing up. Her daughter Cindy was the only one in the family who had the recipe.

"Yep. She got the recipe from Cindy. Betty's gonna give it a whirl."

"Oh, man, this is sounding better and better," Herbert said. "What time do you want me to come over and what can I bring?"

"We will eat around five, and don't bring anything. We have it all planned."

"George, I can't wait. And tell Betty thanks. I feel better already. I mean, I was just going to hang out alone, you know. Thanks, man."

After George hung up the phone he told Betty that Herbert had broken up with Michele. Betty put her thinking cap on immediately. Ever the matchmaker she came up with a plan.

"My friend Virginia! Let's invite Virginia. I think Herbert would appreciate the company."

"Honey, do ya think we should. I mean, Herbie just broke up with Michele a month ago. Do ya think he is ready and on Christmas day?"

"If I know your cousin Herbert, he is ready. Remember the time he broke up with Barbara? Two weeks later he was dating Jennifer. Herbert is ready. He could probably use some cheering up…can't we all."

Betty called Virginia that evening and invited her. She said yes, just like that. Being single she was more than happy to have a family gathering to go to on Christmas day. And Betty let Virginia know that Herbert would be there.

The following two days before Christmas were work days for Herbert. The book store was crowded with last minute shoppers. Herbert was in good spirits. At least he did not have to face the holiday alone. Of course, during these days preceding Christmas, Herbert still had no idea that Betty's friend Virginia would be joining them. It would be a surprise to him. Betty and George did not want to tell Herbert about Virginia. They did not want to put any pressure on him. Had he known that Virginia was going to be there, he would have felt that he was being set up. Not that he would have minded, but it would have put unnecessary pressure on him. Betty and George knew this because they knew Herbert.

Herbert was just expecting a quiet day with his cousins at Christmas. He was happy to have a place to go; his parents were both deceased. So, Herbert was not expecting to be set up when he arrived at George's house on Christmas day. He was not unhappy about it when he found out though, because he wanted to meet someone. He had been with his girlfriend Michele for two and a half years. Herbert felt lonely throughout Fall and into December. Michele had not been around most of the time, which led up to the break up. The holidays were a lonely time for him this year. Work at the bookstore was going well, but Herbert was missing the company of a woman.

Herbert rang the doorbell and greeted George and Betty. Samantha greeted Herbert with her new doll in hand. Virginia had arrived a few minutes before. Herbert was surprised but glad there was a fourth adult to round out the company.

Virginia had long black hair. He always liked long hair on a woman. Herbert found himself immediately attracted to Virginia. Their conversation flowed. While George and Betty were in the kitchen getting things ready for Christmas dinner, Herbert and Virginia were in the den getting acquainted.

Occasionally, Samantha would ask them a question, such as "What's your name?" or "Do you have a dog", but mostly she was busy with her newly acquired Christmas dolls and toys; Linda was busy with a new art kit.

Herbert did not mind that Virginia was two or three inches taller than he. He was ecstatic that he and Virginia hit it off so well. They talked about mutual interests, such as books, plays, movies, and music. Virginia taught sixth grade at St. Francis Catholic School. Herbert wanted to ask her out right away but thought it too soon. Everything flooded his mind at once on what they could do on upcoming dates. In his mind he jumped to a future with Virginia.

Dinner was ready and the table was set. Samantha and Linda were well-behaved, and were preoccupied with their toys and art supplies.

After saying grace the meal began. Betty was a wonderful cook. Aunt Martha's turkey and dressing recipe was a hit. Fresh vegetables out of George's garden accompanied the meal. Desert was something to behold—pumpkin pie, pecan pie, and cheesecake. Herbert was in a good way. Here was a great meal, great company, and a potential future date. This was turning out to be one of the best Christmases he ever had.

The rest of the evening was spent talking with the television on. Linda and Samantha went to their rooms shortly after dinner.

"Let me help with the dishes," Herbert and Virginia said almost simultaneously.

"We will not hear of it," Betty said.

"You two go into the den and make yourselves comfortable. We'll join you shortly," George said.

This plan of George and Betty was to get Herbert and Virginia alone so that they might get to know each other. Herbert followed Virginia into the den. It was a comfortable den. There was a bookshelf across one wall. You would not necessarily find the latest bestsellers here as there were old paperbacks and classics. There were some hunting and sailing magazines strewn about. There was a huge framed picture of ducks in flight at one end of the den and a picture of a clipper ship on the ocean, above the television set. The curtains were of a light green and the carpet was a slightly darker shade of green. A desk sat in a corner with pencils, pens, papers, a dictionary, and an assortment of papers and folders on it.

Herbert always loved their den. He found it cozy without any fanfare or fizz. It was just the right environment for writing and reading and relaxing. He often fantasized that one day when he owned his own house he would like a den like George and Betty's.

Herbert took a seat on the couch and Virginia sat by him.

"So you're a school teacher?"

"Yes, I teach sixth grade over at St. Francis. And you work at the bookstore?"

"Yeah. I work in customer service and I am the booking person for guest authors who come to the store."

"You mean you schedule the authors to come and talk and sign books?"

"Yeah. We schedule an average of three to four authors per month. I schedule them to speak at our store and I send out the PR notices for the newspaper."

"Sounds fascinating."

"We are open tomorrow, of course. You know…day after Christmas shopping and all." There is a pause. "How are the kids at St. Francis?" Herbert asked.

"Good kids. I love teaching there. The staff is wonderful. We have several of the Sisters of the Divine Providence still teaching there. The pastor is excellent. He's such a spiritual man and yet worldly enough to do a great job running the school. He likes to see the lighter side of life. You cannot help but like being around him."

During this social interchange, Herbert was thinking he would like to ask Virginia to dinner for New Year's Eve. The conversation between them was good. But, every time he was about to ask her, he judged the time not right. He kept waiting. But to ask now would interrupt the flow of their conversation, so he waited. In truth, he did not want to risk getting a "no" answer and mess up everything he had going. Timing was everything Herbert had learned from past experiences: you wait too long and you miss. You ask too soon and you miss. The timing has to be just right, and he did not feel it was "just right" yet. Finally, George and Betty came into the room and the opportunity was lost.

"Well, I see you two are getting to know each other," George said.

The four of them watched "It's a Wonderful Life" on television.

"That Frank Capra was one hell of a director," Herbert said.

"One of my favorite movies," Betty and Virginia agreed.

The evening gradually was winding down. Herbert and Virginia said goodbye to George and Betty. George and Betty went back inside (but watched through a crack in the curtains) as Herbert and Virginia continued to talk outside before getting into their cars. For Herbert it was time.

"Virginia, I was wondering…uh,…I hope to see you again."

Herbert knew that he had blown it. He drove home obsessed with thoughts of *Why did I blow it?*

Virginia was left wondering. Being intuitive she knew that Herbert had meant to ask her something but changed his mind. She drove home contented with the evening but wondering what Herbert was going to ask her. She sensed that he was going to ask her something.

The next day found Herbert at work at the bookstore. He had recovered from the previous night's blown opportunity. He was in work mode. It was a bittersweet time for him as he had met a woman he liked and yet there was no future get-together planned.

Virginia was still wondering what Herbert was going to ask her last night. She got dressed, had a light breakfast, and got into her car and drove to the bookstore. She did not know how but she was determined to find out what Herbert wanted.

The store was bustling with customers. Some were spending their after Christmas gift certificates, and some were browsing, happy to be out of their houses from their all day Christmas festivities of the day before. Some were chatting with friends in the coffee shop area. Herbert was helping a bald headed man find books about World War II.

"Yes sir, I will show you where our history books are located if you'll just follow…" Herbert saw Virginia out of the corner of his eye. They made eye contact and she winked. Herbert continued to help his customer. "Follow me sir. Our history section is right over here. And here are the books on World War II."

"Thank you young man," the bald headed man said.

Herbert left the man and walked across the aisle where Virginia was looking at books in the travel books section.

"Going my way?" Herbert said.

"Oh, hi Herbert. I was hoping you would come and talk to me."

"Well, welcome to books."

"Thanks." Virginia paused. She got right to what was on her mind. "Herbert, the reason I came here today is because I sensed that there was something you wanted to ask me. I could be wrong. But if there is something on your mind, feel free."

Herbert was not prepared for this direct communication. He was taken by surprise but he was not rattled. He liked it. He liked her direct attitude. He liked her honesty. The timing was right. Here was his opportunity and he wasn't going to blow it.

"Yes, I wanted to ask you if you were not busy, would you like to have dinner with me on New Year's Eve? That's what I wanted to ask you last night. I kind of lost my train of thought or my nerve. Maybe I felt I was rushing things, I mean, we just met and all. I didn't know how you felt about going out. I just wanted to—"

"Herbert. I cannot go out on New Year's Eve. I have plans to visit my sister for several days in Austin. I'm leaving tomorrow. You know what with school out for Christmas vacation, I have two weeks off. I would go out with you for New Year's Eve except for that."

"Oh ...well, perhaps when you get back we could have dinner?" At this point Herbert was feeling rejected. He threw in this last request not really thinking she would accept. He asked more to lessen the awkwardness.

"Love to!"

He hadn't expected a positive reply. He stood there transformed. Herbert breathed a sigh of relief, and was on Cloud Nine. He showed Virginia around the store. He walked with her to the front of the store. The bald headed man was exiting the store with a book on World War II. She smiled and told Herbert she would call him when she got back to town. He gave her his phone number. He returned the smile.

For this New Year's Eve Herbert was contented to go home and watch the merrymakers in the street in New York City watch ball drop at midnight. He would watch their happy faces, because soon he would be out on a date of his own. Herbert had found a girlfriend. The new year promised to be good.

In Austin there was a woman named Virginia who on New Year's Eve watched the ball drop in New York City on television, and two hundred and fifty miles away there was a man named Herbert who was doing the same thing. The new year promised to be a good one.

NOISE OUTSIDE THE RECTORY

It sounds like a battlefield out there. Firecrackers in the neighborhood. I'm alone in the rectory. Father Ryan and Father Barone are out of town. I'm wide awake. Well, Happy New Year!

NO MORE AIR

It's New Year's Eve. The year's winding down. I can almost feel it, as though the air is being let out of the past year.

ENDLESS POSSIBILITIES

New Year's Eve. I love it whether I'm partying or not.

On past New Year's Eves I've danced, eaten at restaurants with friends, partied, stayed home, watched New Year's Eve on TV, and been lonely.

Anything is possible on New Year's Eve.

TO DANCE OR NOT

There was this dance in town with a live band for New Year's Eve. I thought about going but didn't go. Sixty dollars is a lot for a dance. I stayed home.

Maybe I should have gone.

ABOUT THE AUTHOR

Anthony wrote a monologue and several skits that were performed live on stage in 2022 at Theatre Suburbia in Houston. This is his first book of short stories.

Made in the USA
Coppell, TX
31 July 2023